A Play A

a Dragon

by Steph DeFerie

A SAMUEL FRENCH ACTING EDITION

FOUNDED 1830

SAMUELFRENCH.COM

For Tinki, who liked it best of all.

CHARACTERS

ROLAND – a stage manager
MORTON – a leading man
LADY GWEN – a leading lady
FOLLY – a supporting player
GRUB – a supporting player
LORD MOLLYMOP – a nobleman
LADY DOTTIE – wife of Lord Mollymop
BUD – daughter of Lord and Lady Mollymop
AGNES, BEATRICE, ROBERTA, ROSALIE, MEG –
       would-be actresses
SIR SMALLPART – a knight
KING STANLEY, THE STERN – the king
PINKY – the prince, son of King Stanley
RODNEY, BARRY – guards

The Time: The middle of the Middle Ages

The Place: All over England

SCENES

ACT I

Scene 1: The Great Hall in Lord Mollymop's castle Darkendank, one evening.

Scene 2: The same, the next morning and also a turret atop the castle.

Scene 3: A clearing in the forest, a few days later.

Scene 4: The Great Hall in King Stanley's castle Pilorox (pronounced "Pile o'rocks), that night
and the mouth of a cave in another part of the forest.

ACT II

Scene 1: The Great Hall in Pilorox, the next day.

Scene 2: The mouth of the cave in the forest, immediately following.

Scene 3: The dungeon of Pilorox, that night.

Scene 4: The mouth of the cave in the forest, the next day.

The playwright suggests "The Rob Roy Overture" by Hector Berlioz as pre-show music.

A PLAY ABOUT A DRAGON

ACT I, Scene One

(A small stage in the great hall of Castle Darkendank, Lord Mollymop's castle in the north, one evening in the Middle Ages. The stage faces up so when the actors address their audience, they face away from us.)

(AT RISE: We are presented with the sight of four clothed behinds mooning us! A king (MORTON), a knight (GRUB), a maiden fair (LADY GWEN) and a dragon (FOLLY) are bowing to their, to us, unseen audience to the sound of half-hearted applause. Several pieces of scenery have fallen and only one remains standing. Vegetables lay scattered about. A ragged curtain is jerkily drawn across the front of this stage by ROLAND, the bored and much put-upon stage manager. THE FOUR stand up straight, relaxing, chatting, bickering.)

MORTON.   Again, you fool! Open it again!

(The applause has quite died away but ROLAND dutifully pulls the curtain open again. The cast instantly return to their professional stance — clasping hands and bowing deeply, "mooning" us again. There is very light, tired applause. The "mooning" continues as

7

*MORTON steps upstage out of line to address
his house.)*

MORTON.   Your Lordships, good knights,
gentle ladies, wretched scum. You honor us poor players
with your kind, kind attention. Our hearts thank you from
their very bottoms. With your joy, all sadness is now
behind us. Sorrow is truly at an end. You are as an ass,
butting unhappiness out of this magnificent hall. Can you
hear me, those of you in the rear? *(A "Bronx cheer" noise
answers him.)*   Excellent. And so, from myself, Lady Gwen,
Grub, Folly and Roland...

*(THEY each react to their names and
ROLAND sticks his head in.)*

MORTON.   ...good night, good knights!

*(MORTON bows and there are one or
two claps of applause. A deadly silence descends.)*

MORTON.   *(Hissing.)* Close it, you idiot, close it!

*(ROLAND shuffles across again, drawing the
curtain. The cast stands upright and relaxes once
more. The knight, GRUB, his visor having
fallen down shut over his eyes and gotten stuck,
wanders about blindly, bumping into people and
things and falling over.)*

MORTON.   Wonderful! Brilliant! Another
magnificent performance!

LADY GWEN.   Oh, yes.   Never mind the scenery fell over, you forgot your lines and this fool *(Indicating the dragon.)*   sneezed three times after she was supposed to be dead. You're right - it was a triumph!

FOLLY.   *(Taking the dragon head off her own head.)* It's not my fault! It's dreadfully stuffy in this thing. You try running about with it on *your* head and then holding your breath! At least they get to see *your* face.

LADY GWEN.   *(Indicating knight.)*   And this oaf! He's less than useless! If he steps on my toes one more time...

FOLLY.   *(Examining her droopy tail.)*   Or my poor tail...

LADY GWEN.   I shall kick him in the shins!

(Fortuitously, the knight blunders by right at this moment and steps on everyone's toes or tail. LADY GWEN kicks him in the shins but his armor hurts her foot.)

LADY GWEN.   Owwwwwwww!

(LADY GWEN holds her foot and hops about in pain. SHE grabs onto FOLLY, who grabs on to the knight for support and HE in turn reaches out and grabs the lone piece of scenery still standing.   Scenery, knight, FOLLY and LADY GWEN all tumble to the floor in a heap.)

ROLAND.   *(Joining the group and ignoring the knight and LADY GWEN.)*   That was the worst production of

"Saint George and the Dragon" I have ever seen. And with this company, that's saying something.

MORTON. It wasn't so bad.

ROLAND. Wasn't so bad? The audience didn't laugh or cheer once. It was dead quiet out there.

MORTON. They were *listening*.

ROLAND. They were *sleeping*.

LADY GWEN. *(To knight.)* Get off me!

ROLAND. They threw rotten vegetables at us.

MORTON. *(Picking up some veggies.)* Nonsense! They were simply showing their appreciation by donating the fixings for our supper.

ROLAND. Half the audience walked out!

MORTON. To get their friends for our next show!

LADY GWEN. *(To knight.)* Would you get off of me?!

ROLAND. Did you find nothing wrong with that performance at all?

MORTON. I most certainly did. What was that terribly loud interruption backstage during my great speech?

ROLAND. You mean when I pounded Grub on the back to save his life because he was choking on a chicken bone?

MORTON. *(Covering his ears.)* It completely threw off my concentration and clearly distracted the audience to such a degree, I'm surprised anyone paid any attention to me at all!

> *(ROLAND opens his mouth for a sharp retort but is interrupted before HE can begin. The knight, FOLLY and LADY GWEN*

*have finally gotten themselves sorted out.
FOLLY is now trying to help the knight get his
helmet off.)*

LADY GWEN.   I wish only two things from you,
Morton - keep that fool   *(Indicated the knight.)*   away from
me and give me my pay for the last three years.
FOLLY.   It's only that he can't see.   If we had
proper costumes...
LADY GWEN.   And sets and props and
direction...
MORTON.   You are all so quick to see only the
gloomy side of things.   With the fee from this engagement,
we shall be able to re-outfit ourselves most handsomely.
LADY GWEN.   But will *we* be paid?
MORTON.   What do you need money for, my
dear?   Do I not provide bed and board, every conceivable
need?   Who else stays in Lord Mollymop's own castle, for
goodness sake?
LADY GWEN.   I only want what's owed me.
MORTON.   For what purpose?
LADY GWEN.   To leave.
ROLAND.   What?!
FOLLY.   *(Letting go of the knight suddenly so he falls
over backwards.)*   You want to leave us?
MORTON.   I'm speechless!   I simply do not
know what to say!   What *can* one say to such treacherous
behavior?   Where can one begin...
FOLLY.   Why?   What's wrong with us?
LADY GWEN.   Nothing.   Everything!   It's not
you, it's all of this!   Yes, we're at Castle Darkendank but
we'll be put up in the stables and we'll never be invited
back again.   It'll just be squalid, muddy, little towns and

11

rancid, cold food and freezing beds and threadbare clothing and amateur productions and unappreciative audiences forever.

MORTON. *(Thundering.) Amateur* productions!

ROLAND. And I suppose you're too good to settle for that.

MORTON. *(Thundering.) Amateur* productions!

LADY GWEN. Yes I am too good to settle for that and you should be, as well.

MORTON. You think our productions are *amateur*?!

ROLAND. And what will you do without us? On your own, things will be exactly the same...

MORTON. ...but without the glory!

FOLLY. Is glory another word for stink because I'd be interested in...

LADY GWEN. *(Picking at costume and jewels.)* This isn't glory. It's paint and glass and fakery.

MORTON. And that's beneath you, I suppose, *Lady* Gwen.

FOLLY. How will you find anything better?

LADY GWEN. I shall marry again.

MORTON. Absurd!

FOLLY. Brilliant!

ROLAND. A dream!

MORTON. Who would have you?

LADY GWEN. *(Hurt.)* I have had several proposals since the death of my late husband, Sir Willfred.

MORTON. When you were younger perhaps but let's face it, the years have not been exactly kind...

(LADY GWEN turns away.)

12

FOLLY.   Why don't you push her down and kick her a few times while you're at it?

(FOLLY goes to comfort LADY GWEN.)

ROLAND.   That wasn't very nice.
MORTON.   It's the truth.
ROLAND.   Sometimes the truth is not the most important thing.
MORTON.   Nonsense!
ROLAND.   Of all the things you lack, Morton, none is so dearly missed as tact.

(The knight, GRUB, who has been spending all this time trying to get his helmet off, finally succeeds!)

GRUB.   I think Lady Gwen is very pretty.
MORTON.   You think Ugly Bertha, the witch-hag of Bedford, is very pretty.
GRUB.   She has lovely eyes.
ROLAND.   Lady Gwen?
GRUB.   Ugly Bertha.
MORTON.   Let her leave!   We shall carry on even more triumphantly without her.
GRUB.   Ugly Bertha?
MORTON.   Lady Gwen!
ROLAND.   Then, who shall play the maiden fair?
MORTON.   Folly can do it.
GRUB.   And she was always nice to me.
ROLAND.   Lady Gwen?
GRUB.   Ugly Bertha.

ROLAND. If Folly plays the maiden fair, who'll play the dragon? *(MORTON opens his mouth.)* And don't say me. *(To GRUB.)* And you don't say anything.

MORTON. Why not you?

ROLAND. I have enough to do what with looking after the costumes and the sets and the props and pulling the curtain. I do not have time to be the dragon.

GRUB. I could be the dragon!

MORTON. Grub, you are the brave knight who *slays* the dragon. How can you also *be* the dragon?

GRUB. I could, um . . . or, well, I might sort of...um...you know...

(GRUB lunges about trying to work out how to attack himself. HE ends up on the floor, taking MORTON and ROLAND with him.)

LADY GWEN. Whatever is the matter with Grub? Is he having a fit?

FOLLY. He seems to be trying to kill himself.

LADY GWEN. I think he's touched in the head, I always have. Harmless and eager to please but most certainly touched.

FOLLY. You see what you've done? Grub is going to do himself an injury if you leave us.

LADY GWEN. My mind is quite set and nothing can change it.

FOLLY. You have a definite offer, then.

LADY GWEN. Not as such.

FOLLY. Some interest?

LADY GWEN. Not exactly.

FOLLY. Any hope of getting married at all?

LADY GWEN. *(Pause.)* No.

FOLLY. Then, why...?

LADY GWEN. Because I was married once and I was a lady and I wish to be so again and I never shall be if I stay with this company. And because I wanted to wipe that smile off Morton's face. I wanted him to appreciate me. He takes all of us for granted, Folly. Aren't you tired of it?

FOLLY. Everyone takes me for granted. They always have. Aren't they supposed to?

LADY GWEN. We must all of us stand up for ourselves on our own two feet.

(GRUB, ROLAND and MORTON, tangled together, have almost managed to get untangled and stand on their own two feet when they topple down again.)

(A fanfare.)

VOICE. *(Offstage. Announces.)* Lord Mollymop!

(Enter LORD MOLLYMOP.)

LADY DOTTIE . *(Offstage.)* And Lady Dottie. Must I always announce myself?

(Enter LADY DOTTIE and her daughter, BUD. MORTON, GRUB and ROLAND, still tangled on the floor, bow as best they can. FOLLY and LADY GWEN curtsey.)

ALL. *(Except LORD, LADY and BUD.)* Your Lordships.

LORD MOLLYMOP. I must say, that was a...

LADY DOTTIE. ...vigorous performance. All that lunging and jabbing and running about - it quite wore me out just watching it all.

ALL. Thank you, Your Lordships.

LORD MOLLYMOP. I particularly liked...

LADY DOTTIE. ...that bit where the dragon was menacing the maiden fair. It sent scads of shivers up and down my spine. I grabbed His Lordship's hand and simply crushed it in fright.

LORD MOLLYMOP. *(Holding up a hand.)* I won't be able to...

LADY DOTTIE. ...use it again for a week. I did drop off a bit during the fat fellow's long speeches.

LORD MOLLYMOP. I must apologize if her snoring...

LADY DOTTIE. ...distracted you so I would advise cutting those bits. But all in all, it was a most... *(Groping for just the right word.)*

LORD MOLLYMOP. ...vigorous...

LADY DOTTIE. ...vigorous performance.

ALL. Thank you, your Lordships.

LADY DOTTIE. *(To LORD MOLLYMOP.)* Well, go on. Ask them.

LORD MOLLYMOP. We were wondering...

LADY DOTTIE. ...if we could see that last scene again - the one where the dragon is finally disposed of.

MORTON. That is certainly a very thrilling moment, to be sure, but would not your Lordships more enjoy the scene where I describe...

LORD MOLLYMOP. No, no, just the...

LADY DOTTIE.   ...last one.   That is all that we require.

MORTON.   Very well.

(The ACTORS quickly get themselves ready. LORD MOLLYMOP and LADY DOTTIE settlethemselves on two stools provided by ROLAND.)

MORTON.   Allow me to set the scene.   The wicked dragon Draghignazzo has been terrorizing the kingdom for five score years and ten. Each twelve-month, he demands the fairest maiden in the land be delivered to him. The good King is in despair as this year, it is his own daughter who is to be sacrificed. The dragon menaces the maiden fair.

MAIDEN FAIR.   Oh, who will save me from this blood-thirsty monster? Surely he is sent from the very bowels of hell by the devil himself to gobble me up, body and soul! Where is such a hero who might rescue me and win my undying love?

MORTON.   The King sends the brave knight off with a stirring speech: "Good brave sir knight..."

LORD MOLLYMOP.   Yes, yes...

LADY DOTTIE.   ...skip that bit. Let us get on to the slaying, if you please.

(Enter the knight.)

KNIGHT.   Never fear, maiden fair.   I shall save you!

(The knight and dragon fight and the knight finally wins by running his sword through the dragon. The dragon dies dramatically.)

MAIDEN FAIR.   You have saved me, good sir knight and I am yours!

(The maiden fair throws herself into the knight's arms. He manages to stay upright but only just. SHE kisses HIM, something HE obviously does not enjoy.)

MORTON.   Let us rejoice that now we may...
LORD MOLLYMOP.   No, no...
LADY DOTTIE.   ...none of that.   That is quite enough.

(LORD MOLLYMOP and LADY DOTTIE withdraw a bit to one side. MORTON tries to overhear what they are saying.   BUD shyly talks to THE COMPANY.)

LORD MOLLYMOP.   That is just the sort...
LADY DOTTIE.   ...of thing we need.
LORD.   If we do not...
LADY.   ...send someone to the King by Midsummer's Day...
LORD MOLLYMOP.   ...it will be a very sad Festival...
LADY DOTTIE.   ...and a very sad day for us.

MORTON.   Forgive me for interrupting, your Lordships, but I could not help over-hearing you. Perhaps we might be of assistance?

LORD MOLLYMOP.   You would be willing...

LADY DOTTIE.   ...to go to the King?

MORTON.   For the Midsummer Festival? Most certainly.

LORD MOLLYMOP.   Then you know...

LADY DOTTIE.   ...all about it?

MORTON.   Of course.

LORD MOLLYMOP.   But it would be...

LADY DOTTIE.   ...so very dangerous.

MORTON.   Danger means nothing compared to our desire to please you.

LORD MOLLYMOP.   We are...

LADY DOTTIE.   ...very impressed with your loyalty and bravery.

LORD MOLLYMOP.   Therefore, we charge you...

LADY DOTTIE.   ...with a royal commission. You shall travel with all speed to the King's castle Pilorox and do exactly what you just did.

MORTON.   A royal commission! *(To OTHERS.)* You see? I told you we were a success!

ROLAND.   Forgive me, your Lordships, but there will be numerous expenses...

LORD MOLLYMOP.   Our steward...

LADY DOTTIE.   ...will provide you with enough funds for the journey.

LORD MOLLYMOP.   And we...

LADY DOTTIE.   ...as well as the King...

LORD MOLLYMOP.   ...will reward you...

LADY DOTTIE.   ...most generously...

LORD MOLLYMOP. ...if you...

LADY DOTTIE. ...*when* you...

LORD MOLLYMOP. ...when you...

LADY DOTTIE. ...return.

ALL. Thank you, your Lorships.

LORD MOLLYMOP. But you must...

LADY DOTTIE.   ...arrive before Midsummer's Day.

LORD MOLLYMOP. That is...

LADY DOTTIE. ...of utmost importance.

LORD MOLLYMOP.   We promised very sincerely...

LADY DOTTIE.   ...that someone would arrive by then.

MORTON.   We shall accomplish that most easily, Lord Mollymop. And now, allow me to express our gratitude with a poem I shall compose here on the spot to commemorate this momentous occasion. *(Clears his throat.)* "Your royal beneficence is truly..." What rhymes with beneficence?

LORD MOLLYMOP. Yes, yes...

LADY DOTTIE.   ...that's lovely. We are so pleased. You are dismissed.

(LORD   MOLLYMOP   and   LADY DOTTIE exit.)

VOICE. *(Announces offstage.)* Lord Mollymop!

LADY DOTTIE.   *(Offstage.)* And Lady Dottie, you clot!

BUD. I thought you all did a lovely job.

ALL. Thank you, Lady Bud.

BUD. It must be wonderful traveling about as you do, meeting new people and seeing new things. I wish I could go to Pilorox for the Festival but my parents will not allow it.

ROLAND. It is not an easy road, my Lady, especially for one as fine as yourself.

BUD. I'm sure I could take care of everything. I've had all the training and I hate to see others doing what I cannot. It's very brave of you to go. You don't mind the danger, then?

MORTON. Life is full of danger. We will not allow it to stand in our way.

BUD. I envy you.

FOLLY. You? Envy us?

BUD. Your freedom and your adventure...

LADY GWEN. But you have luxury and comfort, anything you want...

BUD. Except freedom and adventure. I suppose we always want what we cannot have.

FOLLY. I would trade places with you in a minute.

BUD. Would that it were so easy...I wish you all good luck.

ALL. Thank you, Lady Bud.

(BUD exits.)

MORTON. *(To ROLAND.)* Performing for the King at the Midsummer Festival! Think of it! It is a singular honor! There is not a moment to lose. We must advertise immediately for a replacement and rehearse them as we travel. I shall go and cry our opening and you must begin packing the...

LADY GWEN.   Opening for what?

MORTON.   A new actress, of course.   You are leaving us, are you not, my dear?   Off to be married, I believe you said?   *(To ROLAND.)*   If you can get all the costumes...

LADY GWEN.   Oh, I couldn't leave you in the lurch at a time like this.   The least I can do is see you through this final performance.

MORTON.   I wouldn't dream of making you stay a moment longer than you wish.   *(To ROLAND.)*   If you can get all the costumes in the big trunk...

LADY GWEN.   But...but...

FOLLY.   But she's going the same way we are! *(EVERYONE looks at FOLLY.)*   I mean...the man she's going to marry, he lives at Pilorox.   *(To LADY GWEN.)* Does he not?

LADY GWEN.   *(Catching on.)*   Oh! Yes! Yes, he does! Why, he's...he's one of the King's kinsmen.

GRUB.   What an amazing coincidence!

ROLAND.   *(Dryly.)*   Yes, isn't it.

FOLLY.   So does it not make sense that we all travel together for safety and companionship?

LADY GWEN.   I could help the new actress learn my part.

FOLLY.   How nice of you to offer!   Isn't it, Morton.

ROLAND.   It would make things easier.

GRUB.   And the smell when she takes her boots off at night keeps the wild animals away.

(LADY GWEN throws a shoe at GRUB. HE falls over from the smell.)

MORTON.   Very well!   She may travel with us. But I am not chipping in for the wedding present!

(Blackout.)

ACT I, Scene Two

(The stage has been cleaned up and the company is auditioning new actresses.   With doubling, these may all be played by the same one or two women.)

ROLAND.   Next, we have Agnes of York.

(Enter AGNES.)

MORTON.   And what do you have for us today, Agnes?

AGNES.   Well, I can do this.

(AGNES does something odd yet entertaining.)

MORTON.   We'll let you know.

(AGNES exits.)

GRUB.   That was amazing!
ROLAND.   It does put ideas in one's head.
LADY GWEN.   Wherever did she learn to do that?

23

FOLLY.   And why?
ROLAND.   Beatrice of Cumberland.

(Enter BEATRICE.)

MORTON.   What can you do, Beatrice?
BEATRICE.   *(Singing, to the tune of "Greensleeves".)*
There was a swain who loved a lass
With a hey nonny nonny and a nonny ho!
He bowed to her and fell on his...
MORTON.   Thank you!

(Exit BEATRICE.)

LADY GWEN.   It's going to be a very long day.
GRUB.   I quite liked that one.
FOLLY.   You like everyone.
GRUB.   What's wrong with that?
MORTON.   May we please move on?
ROLAND.   Stinky Roberta.

*(Enter ROBERTA.   EVERYONE reacts to
her stinkiness.)*

MORTON.   *(Holding his nose.)*   And what are you
known for, Roberta?
LADY GWEN.   *(Quietly.)*   Besides the obvious.
ROBERTA.   People speak highly of my dancing.

(ROBERTA dances surprisingly well.)

MORTON.   Thank you.   We'll send word.

(ROBERTA exits.)

GRUB.   That was nice.
LADY GWEN.   If you were standing up-wind.
GRUB.   *(Wiping his eyes.)* She made me cry.
FOLLY.   That's the odor making your eyes water.
ROLAND.   Magnificent Rosalie.
MORTON.   *(Hanging his head.)* Oh, no.

(Enter ROSALIE, hobbling with a crutch, as she only has one leg, but we don't see that as she has on a long skirt.)

ROLAND.   What do you do, Rosalie?   Perform magic, play the spoons, stand on your head, squeeze yourself into tiny boxes, walk on stilts, eat fire, touch your tongue to your nose, juggle, perform with a trained bear, wiggle your ears, eat bugs?

(EVERYONE waits hopefully.)

ROSALIE.   *(Triumphantly, as she throws down her crutch and lifts her skirt to reveal that she has only one leg.)*   I tap dance! An-a-one, an-a two –
MORTON.   Alas, we have no call for a one-legged tap dancer.
ROSALIE.   *(Disgusted.)*   That's what they all say.
(Exits.)
ROLAND.   Gwendolyn the Mime.

(Silence and a long pause, as slowly EVERYONE turns to watch for the entrance of GWENDOLYN.)

25

(Offstage a loud thump of someone falling, a brief silence, then another loud thump.)

ROSALIE. *(Offstage. Triumphantly.)* See? I can dance anywhere!

ROLAND. *(Loudly announcing.)* Gwendolyn the Mime.

(From offstage a white gloved hand appears, pauses, begins to perform "the invisible box".)

EVERYONE. *(Immediately yelling.)* THANK YOU!

(Another white gloved hand quickly appears, grabs hold of the first gloved hand, pauses, then obviously yanks the other hand back out of sight offstage. Silence. Beat.)

ROLAND. *(Announcing.)* Blind, deaf and dumb Meg.

(Nothing.)

ROLAND. *(Announcing louder.)* Blind, deaf and dumb Meg!

(Nothing.)

ROLAND. *(Yelling.)* Blind . . . oh, never mind.

(ROLAND exits and returns with MEG, who carries a staff.)

MEG.   *(Stumbling about, shouting.)*   Struck by lightning as a child, can't see, can't hear, don't matter. What do you need, what do you need? I can sing! *(Singing tunelessly.)* "Hey nonny nonny, hey nonny no!"   I can dance! *(SHE stumbles about, off and then on again.)* I can juggle! *(SHE tosses some balls from the pocket of her tunic into the air and doesn't catch one.)* I can tell jokes! Knock, knock!

ALL.   Who's...?

MEG.   How do *I* know? I'm blind! Ha, ha, ha!

MORTON.   I thought you said she was dumb?

ROLAND.   She is. That's the dumbest joke I ever heard.

MEG.   So what do you say? Am I hired?

MORTON.   No, I'm afraid...

MEG.   Good! I'll start packing right away! *(As SHE exits.)* I'll require an egg for breakfast every morning and a new pair of boots and I've always wanted a budgie and a velvet petticoat...

MORTON.   *(Shouting.)* No, thank you! We don't need you! Go away!

MEG.   ...and the finger bone of Saint Jehosaphat. Be right back.

(MEG totters stumbles out.)

LADY GWEN.   Let's be certain to be gone when she comes back.

MORTON.   *(Shouting.)* Thank you!

GRUB.   I quite...

ALL.   ...liked her! We know!

27

MORTON.   Who else have you got?

ROLAND.   *(Reading from a list on a scroll.)*   One-legged Judy, No-legged Martha, Warty Theresa, No-nose Sadie, Berta the Hunchback, Ugly Millicent, Really Ugly Harriet, and Unlucky Samantha.

LADY GWEN.   Oh, that last one doesn't sound so bad. Bring in Unlucky Samantha.

ROLAND.   She used to be known as Lucky Sam until the threshing accident.

(EVERYONE grimaces.)

LADY GWEN.   On second thought, don't bring in Unlucky Samantha.

MORTON.   Is there no one else, then?

ROLAND.   I'm afraid not.

FOLLY.   Perhaps we shall find someone on our journey.

MORTON.   We must hope so. It is best we get started immediately. 'Tis a long trip and we have precious few days to accomplish it. Is everything in readiness?

ROLAND.   All is packed into the cart. We have only to hitch up Patsy and we're off.

GRUB.   I let Patsy go.

FOLLY.   Patsy our horse?

LADY GWEN.   You've let him go?

GRUB.   Roland told me to.

ROLAND.   I most certainly did not.

GRUB.   You did! You said, "Go to the stable, boy, and since we are leaving today, let him go, the horse."

ROLAND.   I said, "Go to the stable-boy and since we are leaving today, let him know, of course."

GRUB.   *(Aside.)* That's not what I heard.

28

LADY GWEN.   So we have no horse to pull our cart?

FOLLY.   Can we not just buy another?

ROLAND.   The money we've been given by the Lord's man is not enough to cover such a large expense.

FOLLY.   *(Disappointed.)* So we're not going?

MORTON.   Don't be ridiculous!   We can pull the cart ourselves.   It's not that heavy.

LADY GWEN.   Oh, *we* can pull it?   All of us?

MORTON.   No exceptions.   Except for those of us with bad backs.   I have a note from my physician.

LADY GWEN.   Surely you don't mean the women?

FOLLY.   Why not?   We're as strong as they are, *(With a look at MORTON.)*   stronger maybe.

LADY GWEN.   You speak for yourself.   I'm a delicate flower a soft breeze might wither.

GRUB.   A flower whose feet are as stinky as a dragon.

(LADY GWEN throws a shoe at HIM. HE falls over from the smell.)

MORTON.   We shall all pull together and enjoy a great success.   Now let us leave here before that horrible woman returns.

(EVERYONE exits. Enter MEG, carrying a bundle and flailing about with her staff.)

MEG.   Hello? Hello? Anybody here? I'm ready to go!   Just point me in the right direction.   Hello? Anybody?

29

(SHE peers about, almost as if SHE can see.)

MEG. Drat! They've gone without me. Never fear, I shall find them again. They can't get rid of Meg that easily!

> *(MEG exits. Lights fade on the main playing area but come up on a small, isolated area - a turret atop the castle. Enter LORD MOLLYMOP, LADY DOTTIE and BUD.)*

> VOICE. *(Offstage. Announces.)* Lord Mollymop!

LADY DOTTIE. And Queen Dottie, mutton head!

> *(THEY enter to stand looking out and down, waving, bidding farewell to our company as they leave the castle.)*
> LORD MOLLYMOP. There...
> LADY DOTTIE. ...they go.
> LORD MOLLYMOP. *(Calling out.)* Fare...
> LADY DOTTIE. *(Calling out.)* ...well!
> LORD MOLLYMOP. *(Calling out.)* Safe...
> LADY DOTTIE. *(Calling out.)* ...journey!
> LORD MOLLYMOP. *(Calling out.)* Good...
> LADY DOTTIE. *(Calling out.)* ...riddance!
> LORD MOLLYMOP. *(Calling out.)* ...luck!
> BUD. Honestly, mother. I don't see why I

can't...

LADY DOTTIE. Bud, we've been over this time and again. You cannot go.

BUD. Please don't call me Bud. I thought I was christened Rosebud.

LADY DOTTIE. You were but that seems so formal. What's wrong with Bud?

LORD MOLLYMOP. I quite like Ro...

LADY DOTTIE. ...Bud. You see? We all like Bud. End of story.

BUD. All right. If you're going to keep calling me that, at least let me go to Pilorox.

LADY DOTTIE. No.

BUD. But...

LADY DOTTIE. But nothing. If you go, the dragon will eat you.

BUD. He won't. I'll kill him first. I've had all the training and my instructors say I'm just as good as...

LADY DOTTIE. Just as good as is not good enough. The King's best men thought they were good enough and look where it got them. Good and dead. It is out of the question for you to go. We said we would send either you or brave warriors to vanquish the monster by the Midsummer Festival and so we have.

BUD. But they're players, not warriors. They'll be eaten.

LADY DOTTIE. That is their choice. No one asked them to go. They volunteered.

BUD. They'll die for nothing.

LADY DOTTIE. Nonsense! They are buying us precious time.

BUD. But the King will simply send soldiers here to take me by force.

LADY DOTTIE. Let him. By then, we shall have fortified the castle and be able to hold him off. It's all very well for the King to say, "Your daughter is the

31

most beautiful maiden in the kingdom, you must send her to the dragon." It's not his child that must be sacrificed. I don't see him sending Prince Pinky to fight the dragon.

BUD.   Pinky wants to but his father won't let him.

LADY DOTTIE.   There! You see!

BUD.   It wouldn't do any good, anyway. He has trouble killing spiders. He'd die horribly.

LADY DOTTIE.   Then the King would know how it feels and drop his request.

BUD.   But if Pinky dies, who will I marry?

LADY DOTTIE.   We'll find someone. You are much too important and beautiful to remain unmarried.

BUD.   But I love Pinky! I don't want anyone else. It's Pinky or no one!

LADY DOTTIE.   *(Running out of ideas.)*   Then you'll be old maid Bud. That's the best I can do. You'll be an old maid but at least you'll be alive. That's better than being poor dead Bud, isn't it?

BUD.   Father, say something!

LORD MOLLYMOP.   If she wants to...

LADY DOTTIE.   This is not an exercise or a game. If she tries and fails, she doesn't dust herself off, take a hot bath and try again tomorrow. She'll be dead. She is not going and that is final!

(LADY DOTTIE exits.)

VOICE.   *(Offstage. Announces.)* Lady...   *(Sound of a crash.)*   Aargh!

LADY DOTTIE.   *(Offstage.)* Oh, shut up!

(BUD looks at LORD MOLLYMOP.)

32

LORD MOLLYMOP. *(In a whisper.)* You have my blessing, Rosebud. I believe in you. Do as you will and Godspeed, daughter.

(BUD hugs the LORD MOLLYMOP. HE exits. SHE remains behind, looking down and thinking.)

(Black out.)

ACT I, Scene Three

(A clearing in the forest. Enter THE COMPANY pulling a two-wheeled cart, as large as can be managed. It is piled up with trunks, crates, set pieces, etc. and has various props, costumes, etc. hanging off the sides. The only one not pushing or pulling is MORTON.)

MORTON. *(Sinking to the ground.)* Stop, stop! By the saints' tears, I can go no further.

LADY GWEN. Poor thing. It *is* tiring watching others work, isn't it.

(THEY stop the cart.)

ROLAND. Might as well make camp here as anywhere. Did we not pass a spring a few moments ago? Grub, take the big pot and fetch some water.

(GRUB takes a large pot from the cart and exits.)

ROLAND. *(Not even looking.)* Other way.

(GRUB re-enters and exits the opposite side. ROLAND, LADY GWEN and FOLLY begin unloading the cart and setting up camp.)

MORTON. And what shall we be feasting on for supper this fair evening? Have we savory meats, exotic fruits, dainty sweets and wines of the rarest vintage to tease our palates?

FOLLY. *(Checking the supplies.)* Three-day-old bread, rancid beef, moldy cheese and the wine's turned to vinegar.

MORTON. *(Wrinkling his nose.)* Delightful.

LADY GWEN. Still so enthused about this little excursion?

MORTON. Merely a temporary condition. We shall receive a noble welcome at Castle Pilorox tomorrow and King Stanley shall be so overwhelmed by our marvelous performance at the Festival that he will shower us with riches and fame beyond measure. We shall forget these petty inconveniences in a snap.

(Enter GRUB.)

ROLAND. Back with the water already?

GRUB. *(Having forgotten what HE went for.)* Water!

(GRUB exits.)

ROLAND. *(Not even looking.)* Other way.

(GRUB re-enters and exits the opposite side.)

MORTON. *(To LADY GWEN.)* You'll be leaving us soon, I expect, my dear. I look forward to meeting your betrothed.

LADY GWEN. So do I. *(Oops!)* I mean, I look forward to meeting him *again*. But you haven't found anyone to take my part. I shall simply have to stay until...

MORTON. No! I wouldn't dream of it! I insist that you leave as soon as...

(Enter GRUB and ROSE, who is BUD in disguise. GRUB is staring at her with a dreamy smile on his face, clearly quite taken with her.)

GRUB. Look what I found!

ROSE. Are you the traveling players?

MORTON. Morton Montesque's Paramount Company of Superior Actors, Master Thespians of Comedy and Tragedy, favored with a royal commission by order of Lord Mollymop to the court of His Royal Majesty King Stanley The Stern...

ALL. ...God save the King!

MORTON. ...Performers of Unequal Talent and Rare Passion, Able to Reduce the Hardest Heart to Tears or Move it to Soar with Laughter.

(Pause.)

ROSE. So are you the traveling players or not?

MORTON. *(Bowing.)* Indeed we are, my dear. Morton Montesque, at your service.

ROSE. Thank goodness! I'm B...Rose and I've been trying to catch up with you for...

35

MORTON.   I swear on the grave of Saint Bersilius I fully intended to pay that bill but we...

ROSE.   No, no. It's not that...

ROLAND.   Don't tell me you're a fan.

LADY GWEN.   Don't let her leave – she's the first!

ROSE.   You don't understand.   I've never seen you perform.

FOLLY.   You don't understand.   People who've never seen us perform are the only fans we'd get.

ROSE.   I've come to join you.

MORTON.   Excellent!   We happen to have an opening as Lady Gwen is leaving us to marry.   You will fit in perfectly.

LADY GWEN.   Shouldn't we try her out first, to see if she can fill my shoes?

GRUB.   Why would she want to do that?   Your shoes are the stinkiest...

(LADY GWEN throws a shoe at GRUB. HE falls over from the smell.)

ROLAND.   Grub, water?

FOLLY.   *(Digging at him with her foot.)*   Yes, Grub Water?

(GRUB exits.)

ROLAND.   *(Not even looking.)*   Other way.

(GRUB re-enters and exits the opposite side.)

MORTON.   Let us play-act for a moment.   Folly, dear, come and do your dragon bit.

(FOLLY collects her dragon head from the cart, puts it on, stands center.)

MORTON.   Now, Rose is it?   Rose, you pretend you are the maiden fair.   That won't be very hard for a pretty young thing like yourself, will it.   Here is a horrible dragon come to eat you.

(FOLLY roars and menaces ROSE.)

MORTON.   Now, what do you do?

(Enter GRUB with MEG.)

GRUB.   Look what I found!
MEG .   Where are we?   *(Clutching GRUB's arm.)* Let me go!   Have I found the players?
FOLLY.   Oh, no!
MORTON.   Not her again!
ROLAND.   How ever did she find us?!
MORTON.   She's like some horrible, wretched curse that will not leave us alone!
MEG .   I've been tramping all over after you, up hill and down dale.   Where have you been hiding?   Forgot about me, did you?   No matter, I've found you again at last!
LADY GWEN.   God's wounds, where did she come from?
ROSE.   Who's that?   Somebody's mum?
LADY GWEN.   I certainly hope not.

37

MEG. *(Swinging wildly with her cane.)* I'm ready! Who am I to play? The lovely young princess? The beautiful queen?

> *(ROSE crosses to MEG, leads her over to one side, sits her on a log or stump and gives her a crust of bread and a drink.)*

ROSE. The poor thing. She needs rest.

MEG. Thank you, my dear. I'll just sit here while you get things ready.

MORTON. If we may return to the audition. Rose, come back and prepare to be eaten by the dragon. Folly, prepare to eat. Grub...

GRUB. I know, Grub, water.

> *(GRUB starts to exit.)*

MORTON. No, no, we need you to rehearse.

GRUB. *(Eagerly.)* The kissing part at the end?

MORTON. No, we're starting before that. The dragon is menacing the maiden fair.

> *(IT does.)*

MORTON. Maiden fair, what do you do?

> *(ROSE grabs a sword from the cart and attacks FOLLY, who runs away screaming.)*

FOLLY. Wait! Wait! Ow!

GRUB. You've got it all wrong!

(GRUB tries to stop ROSE but SHE knocks HIM down.)

ROSE.   Fear not! I shall protect you!
GRUB.   But I'm supposed to protect *you*!
FOLLY.   *(Getting whacked again.)*   No, no!

(ROSE is beating off FOLLY and pushing GRUB back away from danger.)

FOLLY.   *(To GRUB.)*   Help me!
GRUB.   Help *me*!
ROSE.   Die, foul worm!
GRUB.   *(Trying to get a kiss.)*   What about my kiss?

(ROSE notices nothing and inadvertently elbows GRUB in the face.)

FOLLY.   I give up, I surrender! Stop hitting me!
GRUB.   Me, too! I give up, too! Somebody stop her!

(MORTON and ROLAND finally intervene and pull ROSE away from FOLLY and GRUB. LADY GWEN is the only one looking pleased.)

ROSE.   *(Hopefully.)*   How was that?
MORTON.   Such enthusiasm! You certainly threw yourself into it, body and soul.
GRUB.   *(Rubbing a bruise.)*   Mostly body.
ROSE.   But did you like it?
ROLAND.   It was an interesting interpretation.

FOLLY.   You don't mean interesting, you mean painful.

ROSE.   *(Disappointed.)* I didn't do it right.

ROLAND.   Well, it wasn't the way it is usually done.

ROSE.   I'm sorry. I thought I knew everything about it.

MORTON.   No, no. Things like this take much study, that is all.

ROSE.   I'll be leaving you, then.

MORTON.   Tarry a moment. I must address the company.

(ROSE crosses to MEG and puts MEG's hands on her own face so MEG can "feel" her talk.)

MEG.   *(Shouting as usual.)*   Ready to begin, are we?

ROSE.   In just a little bit.

LADY GWEN.   What a dear. Such a shame we have to let her go.

GRUB.   *(Disappointed.)* She's going?

FOLLY.   *(Sarcastically.)* What a loss. Oh, well, time for supper.

MORTON.   Really, must we ask her to leave us, then?

GRUB.   Please don't make her go! She's lovely.

FOLLY.   She's vicious!

LADY GWEN.   We haven't any choice. You saw her. She simply can't act. Roland, what say you?

ROLAND.   'Tis true she played it most unusually...

(LADY GWEN and FOLLY look happy.)

ROLAND.   And yet with more rehearsal and proper direction, I believe she could become a very competent maiden fair.

GRUB.   We would have to do lots more work on the kissing.

(FOLLY hits GRUB.)

FOLLY.   Is that all you can think of?

GRUB.   Yes. What's wrong with that?

FOLLY.   What's wrong is that you don't think of it with...

MORTON.   I would be willing to work with her personally.

FOLLY.   No, no, no! She's hopeless! I vote no.

LADY GWEN.   I would certainly advise against it.

ROLAND.   I do not believe we have much choice.   We must find a replacement for Lady Gwen immediately and there is simply no one else.   It is true she needs practice but she shows much promise.   She has enthusiasm and spirit and a certain look besides.

GRUB.   *(With a sigh.)* She's lovely.

MORTON.   Then it is settled.

LADY GWEN and FOLLY.   But...!

MORTON.   We shall invite her to join us.

(MORTON, GRUB and ROLAND look

41

*pleased. FOLLY and LADY GWEN do
not. MORTON crosses to ROSE.)*

MORTON.   My dear Rose, you show a rare
inclination towards our humble profession. Therefore, we
are pleased to offer you a place in our company.

*(The importance of the occasion is somewhat
marred when MORTON brushes up against
MEG while making a bow and SHE swings
her staff at HIM. It connects solidly.)*

MORTON. Ow! God's wounds!

MEG. Who's that?
ROSE. It is the leader of the company. Don't hit
him. *(To MORTON and OTHERS.)*   Thank you for your
kind offer. I shall try to live up to your expectations and
make you proud of me.

*(ROLAND steps forward with a piece of
parchment and a quill pen.)*

ROLAND.   Here is our roll. Can you make your
mark?

(ROSE signs her name.)

ROLAND. (Shocked.)   You can write?!

(This is a major shock.)

ROSE. *(Lying.)* Yes, a little. When I was a child, we nursed a sick brother on a pilgrimage to Canterbury and he taught me my letters.

MORTON. This is most wondrous! You shall prove a blessed addition to our band. A cheer for our learned ingenue!

MORTON, ROLAND, GRUB. Hip-hip-hurrah!

MORTON. Allow me to introduce ourselves. This is Roland, our stage manager, you've met Lady Gwen, that is Folly and that is Grub.

ROSE. *(Indicating MEG.)* And who is that?

MORTON. I have no idea, but your first task with us is to take her out into the forest and leave her there.

FOLLY. That's the first good idea you've had all day.

LADY GWEN. Here, here!

ROSE. No! How can you suggest such a thing? There are dangerous creatures about.

MORTON. She's the most dangerous thing in here! And I have the bruises to prove it.

ROSE. I will not throw in with anyone so hard-hearted and cold.

MORTON. *(Astonished.)* You refuse to carry out the will of your director?

(LADY GWEN and FOLLY now look pleased. ROLAND and GRUB look stricken.)

ROLAND. The first rule of the company is...

LADY GWEN, FOLLY, GRUB, ROLAND, MORTON. Always obey your director!

ROSE.   Then I shall take her into the forest...

(ROSE helps MEG to her feet.)

ROSE.   ...and I shall not be coming back.
MORTON.   What?
MEG.   Are we going?

(ROSE and MEG begin to exit.)

ROSE.   Yes, you're coming with me.
MORTON.   But where will you go?
ROSE.   Back home, I suppose.   I don't mind taking your orders but I shall not harm anyone.
GRUB.   But she'll be fine on her own. She found us and we left her back at the castle days ago.
ROSE.   She's a poor defenseless creature and I will not abandon her.
LADY GWEN.   She's about as defenseless as a dragon.
ROLAND.   Morton, we need her.
MORTON.   Very well, then. She may stay. But she is your responsibility.
ROSE.   I will watch over her.
ROLAND.   If everything is now finally settled... *(Black look at MORTON.)*   ...can we *please* finish getting set-up?   It will be full dark soon and we have nothing ready! *(Looking at GRUB.)*   Grub!
EVERYONE.   Water!

(GRUB exits.)

EVERYONE.   *(Not even looking.)*   **Other way!**

(GRUB re-enters and exits the opposite side.)

FOLLY. I'll go for firewood.
LADY GWEN. *(Conspiratorially.)* I'll go with you.

(FOLLY and LADY GWEN exit.)

ROSE. What can I do?
ROLAND. You can help me with this shelter, seeing as how Morton has been no help at all.

(ROLAND, ROSE and MORTON busy themselves with trying to raise the tent. While THEY are so distracted, MEG begins to exhibit very odd behavior. SHE watches the others furtively and then begins to quietly creep about, looking and listening. It's as though SHE can see and hear normally! SHE goes through packs as SHE comes across them, taking some small things and hiding them in her cloak. ROSE accidently notices this and watches HER shyly.)

MORTON. Do not despair, my dear. These are not our usual accommodations. We have a royal commission! We have been engaged for the King by Sir Mollymop. Do you know of him?
ROSE. He is lord in the northern lands.
MORTON. He asks that we perform our best piece for the Midsummer Festival at Pilorox - "Saint George and the Dragon." King Stanley will certainly enjoy it.

ROSE.   Perform? You're going to *perform* a play about a dragon?

ROLAND.   What else? We are players, after all.

ROSE.   But...you cannot slay dragons yourself?

MORTON.   *(Laughing.)* Heavens, no! We must leave that to the real Saint George, my dear.   *(With a shudder.)* Real dragons would be quite beyond us.

(LADY GWEN and FOLLY enter, carrying wood, talking and laughing loudly. MEG instantly returns to her place and resumes her act.)

LADY GWEN.   ...and then we shall dunk her in the pond!

FOLLY.   And pelt her with stink eggs! That'll show her!

GRUB.   *(Offstage.)* I've finally got the...

(A tremendous splash offstage.)

GRUB.   *(Shouting offstage.)* God's wounds!

(GRUB enters, soaked, with an empty bucket.)

ROLAND.   Grub?

(GRUB rings out his shirt into the bucket.)

GRUB.   Water!

LADY GWEN.   *(Dropping the wood.)*   There! We've done our bit. When do we eat?

MORTON.   Ask the cook.

46

*(ROLAND and ROSE stand back. The tent
stands for a moment and then collapses.)*

ROLAND.   I cannot do everything!   You lot
work on this and I'll start the supper.

MORTON.   Afterwards, we shall conduct a full
rehearsal and before you know it, we will be at castle
Pilorox and glory!   We shall present our greatest
performance ever!   Nothing between us and everlasting
fame!

(Blackout.)

ACT I, Scene Four

*(The Great Hall in Pilorox, King Stanley's
castle, that night.   The KING is doing
paperwork with a large-plumed quill pen.)*

KING STANLEY.   One hundred gold pieces to
rebuild the mill and forge at Little Chesterwick, fifty gold
pieces for loss of livestock at Paddock-on-Twee, and five
gold pieces for the widows and orphans of Greater
Stableforth. Damned orphans! Do they think my treasury
has no end? Greedy little things! We simply cannot go on
like this!

*(Enter PINKY, his scholarly son, with
a large book.)*

PINKY.   Hello, Father.   What cannot go on?

KING STANLEY.   Hello, Pinky. The chaos and destruction and terror. The cost of it all will ruin me.

PINKY.   There is no need to worry.   Sir Mollymop has promised to send a brave hero by the Midsummer Festival, has he not?   That will end our troubles.

KING STANLEY.   But no one has arrived and the festival is two days hence. The dragon has been offered many beautiful maidens and still he wrecks destruction. Lady Bud is the most beautiful. She is the only one who will satisfy the demon and send him away for another one hundred years. Is that too much to ask?

PINKY.   But I love Bud, Father. You cannot send her to her death.

KING STANLEY.   One maiden to save the whole kingdom. How can we not make that bargain? I must send soldiers to take her from her parents by force. Perhaps I shall also burn his castle to the ground and kill him, his wife, his servants, and his pets as an example to others not to defy my wishes.

PINKY.   Let me face the dragon, Father, please! I'll save Bud and everyone. I'm not afraid.

KING STANLEY.   Oh, Son. What a brave little soldier you are.

PINKY.   It's all right, Father. I'm not scared.

KING STANLEY.   I believe you could do it, my boy. The worm would take one look at you and laugh himself to death.

PINKY.   Please let me try, Father. I know I'll succeed where the others have failed.   *(HE holds up the book.)*   I've been reading up on this sort of thing. I know more about dragons than anyone!

KING STANLEY.   I cannot allow you to go. You are my only heir and you must take over for me when you are strong enough. I cannot risk your life.

PINKY.   But it isn't a risk. I have the love of dear, dear Bud to fight for. I will never give up with that to give me strength and cunning and bravery. There is nothing so terrible that can defeat love.

KING STANLEY.   Oh, Pinky. You are so naive. How could I have failed so miserably in your upbringing?

(Lights fade out on the hall.)

(Lights fade up opposite on the mouth of a cave in the forest. It is a dark, rocky, frightening place, strewn about with bones. A large, low rock with chains attached sits before it. There is a rumble, soft at first, but growing quite alarming. Out from the cave comes a huge, terrifying dragon head and two clawed front legs. [In construction, this is reminiscent of Chinese parade creatures but not so stylized and much more realistic and horrible.] The gruesome jaws open, the eyes roll, smoke pours out, flames shoot forth! There is a terrible roar! SIR SMALLPART enters and fights the dragon. HE loses. There is another terrible roar!)

(Blackout.)

ACT II, Scene One

(The Great Hall in Pilorox, the next day. The company has just finished up a brief explanation of their show to KING STANLEY and PINKY. MEG is skulking about, unnoticed, stealing small things. [A comic bit might be to have her attempt to steal something big.])

MORTON.   ...and then Grub, that's him, fights the dragon.

(GRUB takes a few swipes at FOLLY.)

KING STANLEY.   And he *kills* the dragon?
MORTON.   Of course. Kills it dead.

(FOLLY falls down, twitches extravagantly.)

MORTON.   *(Pointedly.)*   Dead, dead, dead.

(FOLLY lies still.)

KING STANLEY.   *(Looking at GRUB.)*   I must say, he really doesn't look very capable.
MORTON.   I assure you, Sire, he has never failed us before.
KING STANLEY.   And just how many times have you done this before?
MORTON.   More than I can count. And it always goes exactly as planned.

KING STANLEY.   Amazing! Your plan seems needlessly complicated, but you are the masters.

MORTON.   Do not worry.   It will be splendid. You will be most pleased, I guarantee it.

KING STANLEY.   Then my people will honor you all the days of their lives.

MORTON.   We ask nothing more.

KING STANLEY.   But if I am not pleased, things will not go well for you.   My punishment will be swift and severe.   Do I make myself clear?

MORTON.   Certainly, Your Majesty.

KING STANLEY.   Excellent.   *(HE notices ROSE.)*   And who is this lovely creature?

MORTON.   Rose, our newest addition.

KING STANLEY.   You are very beautiful, my dear.

ROSE.   Thank you, Your Majesty.

KING STANLEY.   Perhaps we should feed you to the dragon.

(EVERYONE is aghast.)

ROLAND.   Dragon?

KING STANLEY.   I'm joking, of course.   *(But is he?)*   Where do you come from?

ROSE.   *(Without thinking.)*   The North.   *(Oops!)* ...of the Southlands.

KING STANLEY.   Have we ever met before?

ROSE.   I do not believe...

LADY GWEN.   Do you remember me, Your Highness? Lady Gwendolyn of the Western Marshes?

MORTON.   *(Under his breath.)*   Boggy Swamplands is more like it.

51

KING STANLEY. *(Not paying attention.)* Sorry?

LADY GWEN. I was presented at court when I married my late husband, Sir Willfred. Of course, he wasn't late when I married him. Well, he was late to the ceremony, but...

KING STANLEY. *(Still looking at ROSE.)* Yes, yes, I'm sure. Well, if there is nothing else, Pinky here will show you where to go. Our prayers are with you.

COMPANY. Thank you, Your Majesty.

(KING STANLEY exits.)

PINKY. You came from Lord Mollymop, did you not?

LADY GWEN. He thought...

FOLLY. You mean Lady Dottie thought...

GRUB. We were vigorous!

PINKY. Did you see the Lady Bud?

GRUB. *(With a sigh.)* She was lovely. *(EVERYONE looks at him.)* Well, she was!

PINKY. How I envy you.

FOLLY. You've never seen her?

PINKY. Not once. Father met her during a state visit but all I have is this portrait made when she was 11.

(PINKY takes out a small portrait.)

LADY GWEN. But you are to be married, are you not?

PINKY. Yes, but alas, although we have exchanged letters, I have never, not ever met her myself. Is she well?

GRUB. *(With a sigh.)* She's...

COMPANY. ...lovely!

ROSE. *(From the back of the group.)* Do you love her?

MORTON. Rose! How dare you ask such a thing! Apologize at once for your impertinence!

(ROSE slowly comes forward.)

ROSE. I am very sorry, Your Highness. I meant no offense.

PINKY. It is no matter. I love her with all my heart.

ROSE. And does she love you?

PINKY. Yes.

ROSE. How can you be sure?

PINKY. She has told me so. She tells me thus in every letter.

ROSE. And do you believe her?

PINKY. I do.

ROSE. Then she is the luckiest woman in the world.

LADY GWEN. *(Who has been primping, to FOLLY.)* Have you seen my silver brooch?

FOLLY. No, did you lose it?

LADY GWEN. I thought I was wearing it....

PINKY. I just hope she feels the same when at last we meet. Everyone expects a prince to be big and strong. I'm afraid I am neither.

ROSE. I'm sure that will not matter. She knows you are good and kind and brave and smart. She knows not your face but your heart. Have you not noticed that bees do not always fly to the prettiest flower?

PINKY. Actually, they do.

ROSE. *(Taken aback.)* Oh. *(Brightening.)* Well, women are smarter than bees. Not all women prize beauty or brawn over brains.

LADY GWEN.   Yes, some prefer wealth over everything.

FOLLY. *(Looking at GRUB.)*   And some would settle for any old person if they would just see it.

MORTON. *(To LADY GWEN.)*   So, which sort of bee are you, my dear? Is your intended fair, rich or intelligent?

LADY GWEN. *(Caught off-guard.)*   Oh! Uh...

MORTON. *(To PINKY.)* Lady Gwen is engaged to one of your kinsmen.

PINKY.   Really? I had not heard. Which one? *(A sudden thought.)*   I hope it was not Sir Smallpart!

MORTON. Why?

PINKY. He was killed just days ago.

LADY GWEN. *(Feigning grief.)* No!

PINKY. Were you not told?

LADY GWEN.   We were traveling. *(Sobbing.)* Oh, my dearest, my dear! Where shall I go now, what shall I do?

FOLLY. You'll stay with us, of course.

MORTON.   But we have hired your replacement...

ROSE. That's all r...

MORTON.   ...and I cannot afford to pay two for the same part...

ROSE. But I don't want...

MORTON.   ...and I cannot simply ask her to just leave...

ROSE. I quite under...

MORTON.   ...so you'll have to go.

ROSE.   Master Director, please hear me.   I do not feel I am ready for so important a performance.   I insist you keep the Lady Gwen in her part...   *(MORTON looks disgruntled.)*   ...and allow me to observe her...   *(MORTON looks unhappy.)*   ...and pay me nothing.   *(MORTON brightens up.)*

FOLLY.   Oh, please?

MORTON.   Very well. God alone knows why I allow you to talk me into these things.   You may continue in your part for this final performance.

LADY GWEN.   Bless you, Morton.

PINKY.   And now, we must go so you may prepare.   Follow me.

(PINKY begins to exit.   LADY GWEN catches up to him.)

LADY GWEN.   Your father's a handsome man to be all alone, poor dear.   Has he ever thought of marrying again?

(Fade to black.)

ACT II, Scene Two

(The clearing of the dragon's cave in the forest. There is a low rumbling – the dragon is sleeping in the cave and we can hear the snoring.   Enter THE COMPANY with their cart and

55

PINKY. The cart is parked out of the way. PINKY puts down a bundle of books and his cloak. As the scene progresses, MEG creeps about unnoticed, picking pockets and wallets, stealing things from the cart and the cloak, etc.)

LADY GWEN.   Phew! What a stink!
PINKY.   Shhh!   Wait here a moment and be silent.

(PINKY creeps forward quietly, looking to see if the dragon is at home.)

PINKY.   Good.   He is asleep.   I heard his snoring so I was fairly certain we were safe. Still, it is best to be sure. This is it.
MORTON.   This is what?
PINKY.   Where he lives.
LADY GWEN.   He's not very tidy, whoever he is.

(LADY GWEN picks up a bone, makes to toss it aside, peers at it closely.)

LADY GWEN.   Good heavens! This is a human skull!

(SHE drops it and hastily wipes her hands.)

ROLAND.   Just who does live here?
PINKY.   Why, the dragon, of course. This is his lair. Who'd you think?

THE COMPANY.   Dragon?!   *(THEY begin to exit, making sounds of fear and horror.)*

PINKY.   Shhhhh! He's sleeping! We're safe as long as you make no loud noises. Dragons have poor hearing. Tiny ear holes, you know.
MORTON.   What do you mean, dragon?
PINKY.   Dragon, dragon. Big, green, scales, wings, breathes fire, eats people. Dragon.
ROLAND.   Why do you bring *us* here?
PINKY.   Did you not wish to see it beforehand?
GRUB.   Beforehand what?
PINKY.   Beforehand you...before you kill it.
GRUB.   Kill what?
PINKY.   The dragon.
GRUB.   Who's killing the dragon?
PINKY.   You are...
GRUB.   Who?
PINKY.   You.

(Pause.)

GRUB.   Who?
PINKY.   (Very clearly.)   You.

(A longer pause.)

GRUB.   Wh...?
PINKY.   Is he a simpleton?
FOLLY.   Yes, but why do you believe he is going to kill the dragon?

PINKY.   I'm sorry.   I understood you were the brave heroes come to save us by ridding the land of this foul worm.

MORTON.   Whatever gave you that idea?

PINKY.   Lord Mollymop promised to send someone by the Midsummer Festival.

LADY GWEN.   *(To MORTON.)*   And *we* arrived just in time from the North.

ROLAND.   *(To MORTON.)*   Because *someone* volunteered us.

GRUB.   *(To PINKY.)*   Who's killing the dragon?

MORTON.   I'm afraid there's been a terrible mistake.   We are merely actors *playing* at being heroes.   I volunteered us to perform a play about a dragon.   We can slay no monsters.   So we shall just collect our things and be on our way and leave you to get on with...uh...whatever it is you need to get on with.

(MORTON crosses to the cart.)

PINKY and ROSE.   Wait!

(MORTON stops.   PINKY and ROSE look at one another.)

PINKY.   You cannot go!   There is no one else. If you do not kill the dragon, the King will send his men to Lord Mollymop and take his daughter Bud as a sacrifice.   I will not let her be eaten.   You must help me!

MORTON.   There is nothing we can do.   I'm sure we can explain to the King...

58

PINKY.   He will not believe you.   He is not
called King Stanley the Stern for nothing. He'll think you
were trying to make him look bad.

MORTON.   But it is not our problem.

FOLLY.   But it is!   Now that we know about
poor Bud, we can't just go away and do nothing.

GRUB.   Who...?

FOLLY.   Stop saying that! You don't have to kill
the dragon.

GRUB.   Phew!

FOLLY.   *We* have to kill the dragon.

MORTON. But...

ROLAND.   She's right, Morton. We don't have
any choice.

MORTON.   Yes, yes we do! We have many,
many choices! Let us go far away from here and discuss
them all in great detail!

PINKY.   You are all we have.

MORTON.   We have you, don't we? The young
Prince?

ROSE.   You can't ask him to face the monster all
alone!

PINKY.   *(With a sigh.)*   He's right. I am the
Prince and this is my duty. It would be nice to have help
but I will not command you to stay. I've been reading up
on dragons and I would say I am the world's foremost
authority on them. If there is any way to kill one and live,
I shall find it. All by myself, if I must.

ROLAND.   Is it not only bravery and strength
and skill in combat that is needed?

PINKY.   All those who have stood against the
foul beast before have possessed those qualities and failed.

59

Something else must be required. There is a secret to defeating it and learning will find it out.

MORTON. Then, it is all settled. We're free to go and no hard feelings.

(MORTON begins to exit.)

MORTON. I'll need some help with this cart. If you all could just... *(HE looks back.)* Aren't you coming? God's wounds, nobody move!

ROLAND. What is it, the dragon?!

MORTON. I've lost my signet ring!

LADY GWEN. If this dear boy dies, what are you going to tell Bud?

MORTON. Nothing! I'm never going to see Bud again!

FOLLY. The poor thing! To be a widow before she's even married.

GRUB. And she was so lovely! And you want to feed her to the dragon!

MORTON. I don't want to feed her to anyone. Has anyone seen my ring?

FOLLY. Stuff your ring! You can leave if you want, you great coward, but we're staying.

MORTON. Staying? All of you?

FOLLY, GRUB, LADY GWEN, ROSE. All of us!

MORTON. But...but...it's a real dragon!

ROSE. Soon to be a real dead dragon!

MORTON. Or a real live dragon feasting on a band of poor dead players.

ROLAND. But think of the fame and glory, Morton, when we succeed.

MORTON.   *If* we succeed.   Very well.   If you insist on pursuing this madness, you'd best have a leader with his head squarely on his shoulders.   Besides, I must find my ring.

LADY GWEN.   So, Great Leader, what do we do first?

MORTON.   Well, uhm...

ROSE.   Perhaps we should hear from our dragon expert.

MORTON.   Exactly what I was going to say! Prince Pinky?

PINKY.   Reading about dragons is quite different from observing the real thing.   I would very much like to get a first-hand report on this one.   I'm sure it would reveal a weakness we could exploit.

FOLLY.   If you got close enough to see it, wouldn't it see you, too?

GRUB.   And gobble you up?

PINKY.   Not necessarily.   They have terribly bad eye sight.

LADY GWEN.   *(A bit bored.)*   Fascinating.

PINKY.   *(Thumbing through a book.)*   According to Saint Viscontious, at least.   Terrible sight, bad hearing but excellent sense of smell.

ROSE.   So someone very sly and sneaky could possibly creep up to a dragon and not be noticed.

PINKY.   Possibly.   But they'd stand a better chance if they were covered in dragon snot.

MORTON.   Excuse me.   Dragon snot?

PINKY.   So the dragon wouldn't smell them. The problem is not so much being seen or heard as it is being smelt.   If you smelled just like the dragon, which you would covered in his snot, he wouldn't notice you at all.

    ROLAND.   And where exactly does one find dragon snot?

    PINKY. Anywhere a dragon's been.

(PINKY crosses to a tree and rubs some slime off it. HE makes a face from the smell.)

    PINKY. See? They secrete it and rub it all over things to mark their territory.

    ROSE.   So we find someone who is good at moving about stealthily and quietly without being noticed... *(SHE stands and begins to walk around the group.)* ...and cover them with dragon snot and send them in to spy on the creature.

    PINKY.   It would have to be someone who is very, very sneaky.

    ROSE. Someone who is perhaps... *(SHE pounces on MEG.)* ...a thief?

(EVERYONE reacts with surprise.)

    MEG. *(Shouts.)* Who is that?! What do you want?!

    MORTON.   Here, here. What do you mean, thief?

    FOLLY. I thought she was deaf and blind.

    ROSE. She's no more deaf or blind than you are.

    ROLAND.   I presume you have some proof of this accusation.

    ROSE.   I've been watching her. Check your packs and see if anything is missing.

(ROSE *begins searching* MEG. *The* OTHERS *check their packs.*)

MEG.   What are you doing? Help! Robbers! Picking on a poor deaf and blind woman!   *(Sudden laugh.)* Not there - I'm ticklish!   Is this some wicked torture? *(Another laugh.)*   Not there, either - you'll tickle me to death!

LADY GWEN.   I missed my silver broach this morning.

FOLLY.   My ivory comb is missing!

MORTON.   My signet ring...

ROLAND.   The company funds are gone.

LADY GWEN.   Company funds? There were company funds and we never got paid?!

ROSE.   Your Highness?   Do you miss any property?

PINKY.   The gold clasp from my cloak has been torn off.

ROSE.   *(Dropping things from* MEG *into a pile.)* Clasp, comb, broach, coins, ring. It's all here.

MEG. Help! Robbers!

ROSE.   You may stop pretending, thief.

MORTON.   Why would you do such a thing, you ungrateful wretch?

ROLAND.   Think about it - what a clever scheme! No one would pay attention to her and she would be free to see where all the valuables were hidden. No one would suspect her when something went missing. And she could steal a fortune, picking the pockets of the crowds at our shows.

MEG.   *(Pretending to sob.)* Help, help!

(ROSE shakes MEG.)

ROSE. Stop that now. Your act is finished.

(MEG stops pretending.)

MEG. What will you do with me?

PINKY. We shall turn you over to my father for punishment.

MORTON. I say we hang her here and not bother your father at all.

ROSE. Wait! We can use her. She can go into the cave and spy on the dragon.

MEG. Never in a million years.

ROSE. You can spy on the dragon or rot in the King's dungeon until he decides to hang you. At least this way, you stand a chance of escaping with your life.

MEG. A very, very, very, very, very small chance.

ROSE. You have no chance at all of escaping the noose.

MEG. *(Considering.)* True. But if I do this, you must pardon me all my crimes and set me free.

PINKY. That is beyond my power but I will speak to my father on your behalf.

MEG. No deal.

ROLAND. What about treasure? Do not dragons keep a store of gold and jewels in their caves?

MEG. Keep talking.

ROSE. You may keep as much as you can carry out.

MEG. I'm your girl.

(PINKY and MEG shake hands. ROLAND gets a torch and lights it with a tinderbox. MEG gets a sack from the cart. PINKY collects snot from the trees.)

PINKY. Time to grease you up.

(PINKY slathers the slime on MEG.)
MEG. *(Making a face.)* Phew! I should get extra for this, covered in dragon snot.
PINKY. It's for your own protection. You'll be perfectly safe as long as you make no noise. Look at everything closely and remember what you see.

(MEG crosses to the cave, taking the torch.)

MEG. Might I have a sword to defend myself?
PINKY. It would do you no good. You lack the strength to pierce the thick, scaly hide.
MEG. Dear God, please watch over this poor, humble sinner and deliver her safely from the monster's den. Amen. *(SHE crosses herself.)*
LADY GWEN. Are you religious?
MEG. I am now.

(MEG slowly enters the cave. Since the side of the cave is made of scrim, with a change of lighting, we can see what's happening inside. The DRAGON is stretched out, fast asleep. MEG creeps about, slowly and quietly, takes a quick look around, finds a pile of loot, grabs some and puts it in her sack. The DRAGON almost wakes up. MEG freezes. The DRAGON

65

*snorts, sniffs her, finds nothing amiss, falls back
into a deep sleep. MEG starts to leave but her
cloak catches on the dragon's scales! SHE
panics, pulls it free in a frenzy and then hurriedly
leaves the cave. It fades into darkness once
again.)*

MEG.   Am I still alive or have I died of fright and
gone to heaven?
MORTON.   If you are here, it most certainly isn't
heaven.
PINKY.   What did the dragon look like?
MEG.   Horrible! Snoring away, the big, fat, soft
belly heaving up and down with each snort! I'm getting as
far away from here as quick as I can!

(MEG starts to exit.)

ROSE.   Wait! Did you not see anything unusual,
then?
MEG.   It's a dragon! It's all unusual!
GRUB.   So we still don't know how to kill it?
MORTON.   And we never will. I suggest we al
leave at once before it wakes up and devours us in a
instant.

(The COMPANY crosses to the cart.)

PINKY.   I was so sure something would come c
it.
ROSE.   Do not despair. It was a good ide
Perhaps, next time, you might go your...

*(Enter KING STANLEY and two guards,
RODNEY and BARRY.)*

KING STANLEY.   Pinky! I heard you were here. What on earth are you doing?

PINKY.   All is well, Fa...

KING STANLEY.   I will not have you putting yourself in danger. You're all I have left, now that your mother is dead. Please leave. What is that horrible smell?

PINKY.   But I can help them destroy...

KING STANLEY.   There is no need for that now. I have solved the problem. You are all dismissed.

(The COMPANY bows.)

COMPANY.   Thank you, Your Majesty.

*(A gold pin falls from MEG's garments.
KING STANLEY picks it up.)*

KING STANLEY.   Pinky? Is this not the pin your mother gave you on your fifth birthday?   Thief! Guards, arrest her at once!

*(The GUARDS produce chains and manacles
and bind MEG's hands.)*

MEG.   No, no! Your Majesty, there is a mistake! Your son...

KING STANLEY.   We will hang you later. Right now, I must save my kingdom. What is that smell? *HE turns to ROSE.)*   I have had a letter from Lady Dottie of the North. She fears Lady Bud has done something foolish and traveled here in disguise. What do you think?

ROSE. I'm sure I don't know, Your Highness.

KING STANLEY. Ah, but I think you do. You are different from these others, the way you think and speak and act.

ROSE. Your Majesty, I believe you are mistaken.

KING STANLEY. Am I? Come, come, let us pretend no more. You are the Lady Bud, are you not?

(EVERYONE reacts to this. Consequently, MEG is now pushes to one side, completely ignored. SHE takes the opportunity to pick the lock on her manacles and exit.)

PINKY. Rose? It this true?

GRUB. Rose is really Lady Bud?

MORTON. I always suspected as much!

ROLAND. That's why she can read and write!

FOLLY. *(Pleased that BUD is out of GRUB's reach.)* A noblewoman!

LADY GWEN. *(Also pleased that her place in the company is secure.)* She's a noblewoman!

PINKY. Why didn't you tell me?

BUD. I was afraid you wouldn't like a girl who likes to fight dragons and send me back.

KING STANLEY. *(To GUARDS.)* Seize her!

(The GUARDS grab BUD and manacle her hands.)

PINKY. Father! What are you doing?

KING STANLEY.   Saving my people.   The dragon demands the fairest maiden. He shall have her.

PINKY. Father! No!

KING STANLEY. Just one life to buy peace for the entire kingdom for one hundred years. It is a fair bargain.

PINKY. As long as that life isn't mine.

KING STANLEY.   Be quiet, Pinky. You're a Prince. Royalty is different.

PINKY. But it shouldn't be!

LADY GWEN. You're not going to feed her to the dragon!

KING STANLEY. I most certainly am.

GRUB. But she's lovely!

BUD. Everyone, please. This is what must be. We can't find any way to kill the thing and I do not wish anyone else to suffer if I can stop it.

PINKY. I won't let you sacrifice yourself!

KING STANLEY.   It isn't up to you. Tomorrow is the Midsummer Festival and the dragon is expecting a beautiful snack. I'm going to give it to him. *(To GUARDS.)* Take her to the dungeon. She may have tonight to say her prayers and write her parents. By this time tomorrow, it will all be over. *(To BUD.)* It's nothing personal, my dear. *(To GUARDS.)* Take her away.

(The GUARDS exit with BUD.)

KING STANLEY. *(To the COMPANY.)* Thank you for bringing her to me.

(KING STANLEY exits.)

69

PINKY. Bud! Bud! We must save her!

MORTON. She'll be chained up in the dungeon surrounded by guards. We don't stand a chance.

PINKY. We've got to try. I can't lose her just now that I've found her.

LADY GWEN. Don't worry, dear. We'll get her out.

FOLLY. Of course we will.

MORTON. *(Sarcastically.)* Why wouldn't we?

GRUB. She's much too lovely to eat.

ROLAND. Perhaps our thief could...where is she?

(EVERYONE looks around but MEG is quite gone. The manacles are laying on the ground.)

MORTON. She's gone!

PINKY. It is no matter. Let her go. We have bigger problems to worry about now.

MORTON. Bigger, greener and hungrier.

(ALL exit. The DRAGON comes out from his cave and looks about, suspiciously.)

(Blackout.)

ACT II, Scene Three

*(The dungeon in Pilorox, or just a large cage in
the Great Hall late that night. BUD is inside
but unchained. Perhaps SHE sits on a stool.
Enter THE COMPANY with KING
STANLEY and two GUARDS, RODNEY
and BARRY.)*

BUD.   You came! I'd hoped...But, you are not in
any trouble yourselves?

PINKY.   No, no.   We just wanted to...say
goodbye.

LADY GWEN.   *(Flirting with the KING.)*   It's
very kind of Your Highness to allow us this visit.

KING STANLEY.   I am in your debt for
bringing Lady Bud to me.

LADY GWEN.   A great leader such as yourself
cannot be too careful.   But you can see we are quite
harmless.

*(LADY GWEN lifts her skirts a little bit,
showing off her ankles. KING STANLEY
looks at them appreciatively. GRUB, staring at
BUD in admiration again, trips or walks into
the KING.)*

LADY GWEN.   *(Angered that her ploy has been
interrupted.)*   Some more harmless than others.

KING STANLEY.   Responsibility is a heavy
burden I take very seriously.

71

LADY GWEN.   Thank goodness you have such wide, strong shoulders to bear it.

KING STANLEY.   *(Flattered.)*   It is kind of you to notice.   You are certainly more observant than your comrades.

LADY GWEN.   I am not at all like my comrades. I am a noble-born lady who is used to the finer things.

KING STANLEY.   What calamity brought you down thus?

LADY GWEN.   My beloved husband, God rest his soul, was eaten by his horse and there were numerous debts so I was forced to...

(LADY GWEN leads KING STANLEY and the GUARDS off, chatting away gaily. SHE signals behind her back to THE COMPANY.)

ROLAND.   Now we may talk freely, thanks to Lady Gwen's ankles.

MORTON.   Oh, yes.   Let's all thank her for once again reminding us that she's better than us.

FOLLY.   She doesn't think that.   It's all in your head.   Is that why you're so anxious to get rid of her?

MORTON.   Always holding her title up over our heads and rubbing our noses in it...

GRUB.   How can we rub our noses in it if it's up over our heads?

FOLLY.   She's doing us a favor getting that cold-hearted villain away so we can talk priv...   *(Realizing PINKY is the villain's son.)*   Oh, sorry, Your Majesty.

72

PINKY. That's all right. I know he's not the best king. He's been ever so cold and bitter and hard-hearted since Mother died. But he means well.

ROLAND. He's going to feed your fiancée to a dragon and he means well?

PINKY. He just wants to stop all the destruction.

BUD. The only way to do that for good is to kill it.

FOLLY. But we don't know how.

MORTON. Not for lack of information.

ROLAND. We've gone over everything Prince Pinky knows about dragons all afternoon long.

BUD. Then, we must go over it again.

(A general wail of anguish from THE COMPANY.)

PINKY. But I've told it a hundred times already.

BUD. Then tell it a hundred and one. If you know everything about dragons, then you know the answer. We just have to find it.

FOLLY. I'm sick to death of dragons! If I have to hear one more time all those horrible details about when they sleep and how they mate and what they eat and how much they poop, I'll scream!

GRUB. *(Staring at BUD.)* I could sit here and listen all day.

FOLLY. What are we talking about, then?

GRUB. *(Dreamily.)* Dragon poop. It's lovely.

(FOLLY hits HIM.)

PINKY. I wish I could come up with the answer.

BUD. You will. I know it. Anyone who's read as much as you...

PINKY. But what good is that? It isn't helping us at all. All my smart brains and I can't defeat a great crawling, smelly worm.

MORTON. Smelly is right. We're over five leagues away from his cave and I can still smell the filthy thing.

FOLLY. At least it must be easy for them to find a date, the lucky buggers, being so stinky.

PINKY. Not really. Dragons are scarce and if they want a mate, they need all the help they can get. They sniff each other out and rear up on their hind legs in a sort of courting dance.

MORTON. We know!

GRUB. How can you tell which is a boy and which is a girl?

MORTON. Really, Grub, if you don't know that by now...

GRUB. I mean dragons!

PINKY. The males are smaller. And then there are the stomachs. The females have great, soft stomachs.

BUD. Why?

PINKY. Because they're the ones who lay the eggs. If a male with all those sharp, hard scales on his belly tried to sit on a nest of eggs, he'd smash them to pieces.

ROLAND. This is all very interesting...

MORTON. No, it isn't.

ROLAND. ...but it isn't getting us anywhere.

GRUB. If only that thief lady had had a sword when she went into the cave, it'd be dead by now and Rose would be safe.

BUD.   I wonder what's happened to her.   I suppose she'll go back to pretending to be...

PINKY.   *(To GRUB.)*   What?   What did you say?

GRUB.   Nothing.   I was just thinking...

ROLAND.   That's a first.

MORTON.   Grub, how many times have I told you not to bother the grown-ups while we're talking?

PINKY.   No, no!   Grub, it's all right.   Tell me what you said.

GRUB.   Just that everything would be fine now if the lady had possessed a sword.

PINKY.   But she wasn't strong enough to push it through that tough hide.

GRUB.   She wouldn't have had to.   She said there was a great, soft belly.   I remember because it reminded me of Morton's great, soft belly, and when you said that about it being a female, I thought Morton should be a female...

PINKY.   I missed that!   So she's a girl!

GRUB.   *(Patiently.)*   No, Morton's a boy.   See, he has a little...

BUD.   You mean the dragon!   The dragon's a female!

GRUB.   Hooray!   *(Pause.)*   But what good does that do us?

FOLLY.   Male, female, they always keep their bellies low to the ground you said.

PINKY.   Except when they're courting!   Grub, I could kiss you!

GRUB.   All right.

PINKY.   *(Kissing GRUB.)*   You've solved it!

BUD.   You have an idea!

PINKY.   Yes.   But we will need courage and strength and a good strong arm.

BUD. I have enough for all of us.

PINKY. We will have only the one chance.

BUD. That is all we need.

FOLLY. But you're a prisoner! You can't help us locked up in here.

PINKY. And Father will never let you out.

ROLAND. Then we shall have to break her out.

BUD. But all the guards...we'd never make it...they'd catch us before we reached the moat.

FOLLY. Not if they didn't know you were gone.

GRUB. How could she be gone if she's not gone?

FOLLY. If I stay in her place and pretend to be her.

BUD. I can't let you do that!

FOLLY. But we need you to kill it. I can't do what you can.

BUD. But...

FOLLY. If we can't kill it, you'll get eaten and it'll come back in one hundred years and eat more maidens. If you can kill it now, and you're the only one who can, it'll never harm anyone again.

GRUB. You're going to let the dragon eat you?

FOLLY. Of course not! You're going to kill it before it eats me. You better.

BUD. No, it's out of the question.

FOLLY. You are willing to sacrifice yourself. Am I not good enough to do the same?

(Pause.)

BUD. Then we'd better change clothes.

(BUD begins taking off her cloak.)

GRUB.   Folly, no! You can't! What if something goes wrong?

FOLLY.   It won't. You make sure it doesn't.

GRUB.   We can't...we can't lose you!   You're lovely! I never realized it until right now this very minute but you are!

FOLLY.   You think everyone's lovely.

GRUB.   But you really, truly are! I'll do it!

FOLLY.   You'll do what?

GRUB.   Pretend to be Rose!

FOLLY.   Don't be silly! You don't look anything like...

GRUB.   You can make me up and give me a wig and they'll never know!

(Pause.)

ALL BUT GRUB.   It'll never work!

GRUB.   It must work! Please let me try!

(EVERYONE looks at each other.)

PINKY.   What's the worst that could happen?

MORTON.   That they find out and throw him in the dungeon?

GRUB.   And that's where I am anyway!

ROLAND.   Are you sure you want to do this, Grub?

GRUB.   Can't I have a chance to be a real hero, not just a play one, just this once?

FOLLY.   A real hero is one thing but a dead hero is quite another.

GRUB.   I won't be dead.   *(To BUD.)*   You'll kill the dragon before it eats me.   Promise.

BUD.   I will.   *(SHE kisses him.)*   Thank you.

(FOLLY grabs GRUB and gives HIM a huge kiss. HE is quite dazed.)

GRUB.   We'll be right back.

BUD.   I'll be here.

GRUB.   Of course you will because you're a prisoner and you can't...   *(The penny drops! HE smiles.)*   Oh! *(To the others.)*   It's a joke!

MORTON.   *(Sarcastically.)*   Oh, yes.   What could possibly go wrong with this plan?

(Blackout.)

ACT II, Scene Four

(Enter RODNEY and BARRY, the two guards, and GRUB, dressed in BUD's clothes with a wig on his head and make-up on his face. His hands are manacled in chains. THEY cross to the rock and the GUARDS prepare to chain GRUB to it.)

RODNEY.   So this is the most beautiful maiden in the kingdom, eh?

BARRY. That's what they say.

RODNEY. *(Taking a close look at GRUB.)* I don't see it.

GRUB. *(Slapping RODNEY's face and speaking in a falsetto.)* Fresh!

BARRY. You're not a dragon. Maybe this is just what a dragon finds beautiful.

RODNEY. Maybe the dragon's blind.

GRUB. *(Slapping RODNEY's face, speaking again in falsetto.)* Fresh!

BARRY. It's not the look of the maiden, it's the taste. She must taste beautiful.

RODNEY. You think?

(RODNEY kisses GRUB.)

GRUB. *(Slapping RODNEY's face, speaking in falsetto.)* Fresh!

(RODNEY and BARRY chain GRUB to the rock.)

BARRY. We'd better go. *(HE looks at the cave nervously.)* I have a weak stomach.

(BARRY exits.)

RODNEY. Look me up if you survive this, sweetie.

GRUB. *(Shouting after.)* Fresh!

(RODNEY exits. Enter THE COMPANY
and PINKY.   BUD is dressed in GRUB's
clothes.)

FOLLY.   Grub! Are you all right?

GRUB.   I think so. I feel...

BUD.   Scared?

ROLAND.   Anxious?

MORTON.   Nervous?

GRUB.   Pretty!

MORTON.   We'd better get him back into his own clothes as soon as possible.

GRUB.   Did you build it?

FOLLY.   Wait until you see - it's perfect!

LADY GWEN.   No lady dragon could resist it.

PINKY.   If this doesn't make our monster stand up and take notice, nothing will.

BUD.   One clear shot at that great, soft belly is all I need.

(There is a low growl from the cave.)

ROLAND.   She's waking up!

MORTON.   Show time!

FOLLY.   Be brave, dear Grub. We're going to rescue you and everything will be all right.

GRUB.   It better be. If I get eaten, I'm going to be very angry.

(The roar grows louder.)

PINKY.   This is it! Battle stations, everyone!

(THE COMPANY and PINKY exit at a run. Smoke puffs out from the cave.)

GRUB.   Wait! I've changed my mind! Maybe this wasn't such a good idea after all!

(Enter THE COMPANY opposite the cave. THEY are pushing the cart before them. The figure of a rearing dragon has been attached to the front of it with FOLLY's costume head on top. BUD is guiding a long lance which runs along the cart's side. At the moment, it is retracted so it does not stick out.)

PINKY.   Get ready!

(The dragon emerges from the cave. Unfortunately, GRUB is now between the cart and the dragon.)

FOLLY.   Wait! We've made a mistake! Grub is in the way!
LADY GWEN.   How are we going to get him out of there?

(Enter MEG at a run. SHE crosses to GRUB and begins to work on picking the lock on the chains.)

MEG.   Diversion! I need a diversion!

(FOLLY runs out from behind the cart to one side of the cave and begins waving her scarf.)

FOLLY. Here! Over here!

(The dragon shifts its attention to FOLLY for a moment then back to GRUB.)

FOLLY. *(Tantalizingly.)* Look at me! Don't I look delicious?

(The dragon is torn between FOLLY and GRUB.)

MEG. Don't worry, Rose, I'll get you... *(SHE realizes it isn't ROSE.)* You're not Rose!
GRUB. Thief! Help! Thief!
MEG. I *am* trying to help you, you idiot! Hold still!
BUD. Hurry!

(The dragon turns its attention back to GRUB.)

FOLLY. You don't want to eat him! Tough and stringy and disgusting!
GRUB. *(Offended.)* Here! There's no call for that kind of talk!

(MEG has picked the lock and GRUB is free.)

MEG. Run!

(MEG and GRUB run back to the cart. The dragon snaps at them but misses.)

BUD.   Folly!   Run!   Get out of the way!

(The dragon turns its attention back to FOLLY. SHE is hypnotized by it, frozen in fear.)

LADY GWEN.   She's too scared to move!
PINKY.   And the dragon's not looking at us at all!

BUD.   *(To the dragon.)*   Stand up!   Stand up!
PINKY.   It's no use, she's not interested in us!

(LADY GWEN gets an idea.)

GRUB.   Why's she so taken with Folly?
BUD.   No!   Oh no!   We've been wrong all along! *Folly* must be the most beautiful maiden in the kingdom!
MEG.   She's doomed!
PINKY.   We'll never get the monster's attention now!
BUD.   If we can't get a shot at the unprotected belly, we're doomed!

(LADY GWEN takes off her shoes and hangs them onto the cart. The dragon, ready to eat FOLLY, stops and sniffs the air.)

MORTON.   What's she doing?
ROLAND.   She smells something, something even worse than herself!

GRUB. Lady Gwen's shoes!

(The dragon turns its attention to the cart.)

PINKY. It's working! She's interested in us!

(The dragon finally rears up at the cart, exposing its stomach.)

BUD. Now!

(GRUB runs out and tackles FOLLY to the ground. BUD pushes out the lance so it sticks out from the front of the cart. THE COMPANY and PINKY and MEG run the cart forward. BUD guides the lance and it pierces the DRAGON's soft stomach. Big reaction from the dragon! It roars, thrashes about, etc. THE COMPANY hold on to the cart and lance with all their might. FOLLY and GRUB huddle out of the way. Finally, the DRAGON slumps down. The lance is withdrawn. The dragon falls to the ground.)

LADY GWEN. *(Whispering.)* Is it dead?

(PINKY crosses to the dragon.)

BUD. Careful!

(PINKY prods the body. It jumps in one final death shudder. EVERYONE jumps in surprise!)

MORTON. Look out!

PINKY. *(Kicking the body.)* No, it's all right. It's dead now, really dead. *(HE kicks it again.)* See?

(FOLLY and GRUB get up.)

FOLLY. We did it! We killed the dragon!

GRUB. And you're the most beautiful maiden in the kingdom.

FOLLY. Who knew?

BUD. *(To MEG.)* Why did you come back?

MEG. You were the only one ever treated me kindly. I couldn't stand by and see you eaten by that thing.

PINKY. You have earned a full pardon by your bravery.

MEG. But your father...

PINKY. ...will not be king any longer. Now that we have defeated the dragon, I have proven myself worthy and may ascend to the throne. It is time for him to retire and the kingdom to enjoy a new era of...uh...

ROLAND. Compassion?

BUD. Benevolence?

GRUB. Niceness?

PINKY. *(To GRUB.)* Exactly.

LADY GWEN. I could get used to the life of a retired monarch. *(To PINKY.)* You might put in a good word for a tired lady with pungent feet. A wife is just what your father needs.

PINKY. *(Smiling.)* Of course. Your feet, not to mention your brains, deserve to be rewarded. And a wife is just what I need as well.

BUD. But should you not marry the most beautiful maiden in the kingdom?

PINKY. I don't want her. I want you.

BUD. Then, I am yours.

ROLAND. And we have lost a very promising player.

MORTON. *(Nudging GRUB.)* Don't you have something to say? *(GRUB considers.)* To a certain young woman, perhaps?

GRUB. Oh, yes! *(To MEG.)* Thank you for rescuing me.

MORTON. Grub, you are truly hopeless.

ROLAND. Isn't there another young woman...

GRUB. Of course! *(To BUD.)* Thank you for killing it.

ROLAND. Morton is right. You are hopeless.

PINKY. There is someone else, I think.

GRUB. I forgot! *(To LADY GWEN.)* Thank you for your stinky feet. I'll never make fun of them again.

LADY GWEN. What about Folly? Remember her?

GRUB. I can't talk to her. She's the prettiest maiden in the kingdom. What would she want with me?

LADY GWEN. Why don't you ask her? You might be surprised.

(GRUB turns to FOLLY.)

GRUB. I know I'm not much. But I'll love you as hard as I can, better than anyone else in the whole world.

FOLLY. *(Fondly.)* Big talk from a fellow in skirts. *(SHE kisses HIM.)*

ROLAND. *(To MORTON.)* I guess that leaves you and I.

MORTON. That's comforting.

MEG. What about me? Care to make an honest woman out of a devious thief?

MORTON. I don't think so.

ROLAND. Admit it, Morton. She's the finest actress you've ever seen. She fooled you good.

LADY GWEN. And there will be an opening once I'm married.

PINKY. And she has the treasure from the cave.

ROLAND. Or would you prefer Rank Rosalie?

MORTON. *(To MEG.)* You're hired.

MEG. *(Shaking his hand.)* You won't regret it.

MORTON. I already do. *(Smelling his hand.)* Can't you wash that stink off any better?

PINKY. So, Master Thespian, what play will you give us at the Festival tonight? I trust you have had enough of monsters?

MORTON. Certainly not! We shall have a wonderful piece—totally new, never before seen and every word true, every word! "The Players Versus The Devil's Worm!" It is full of humor and excitement and thrills, danger and laughter and true love. What more could you ask for? It is...a play about a dragon!

(Blackout.)

* * *